WELCOME TO
PASSPORT TO READING
A beginning reader's ticket to a brand-new world!

Every book in this program is designed to build read-along and read-alone skills, level by level, through engaging and enriching stories. As the reader turns each page, he or she will become more confident with new vocabulary, sight words, and comprehension.

These PASSPORT TO READING levels will help you choose the perfect book for every reader.

READING TOGETHER
Read short words in simple sentence structures together to begin a reader's journey.

READING OUT LOUD
Encourage developing readers to sound out words in more complex stories with simple vocabulary.

READING INDEPENDENTLY
Newly independent readers gain confidence reading more complex sentences with higher word counts.

READY TO READ MORE
Readers prepare for chapter books with fewer illustrations and longer paragraphs.

This book features sight words from the educator-supported Dolch Sight Words List. This encourages the reader to recognize commonly used vocabulary words, increasing reading speed and fluency.

For more information, please visit passporttoreadingbooks.com.

Enjoy the journey!

Little, Brown and Company

Hachette Book Group
1290 Avenue of the Americas, New York, NY 10104
Visit us at lb-kids.com

Little, Brown and Company is a division of Hachette Book Group, Inc.
The Little, Brown name and logo are trademarks of Hachette Book Group, Inc.

The publisher is not responsible for websites (or their content) that are not owned by the publisher.

First Edition: April 2017

Library of Congress Control Number: 2016948008

ISBNs: 978-0-316-31885-3 (pbk.), 978-0-316-31884-6 (ebook), 978-0-316-55375-9 (ebook), 978-0-316-55371-1 (ebook)

10 9 8 7 6 5 4 3 2

CW

Printed in the United States of America

Passport to Reading titles are leveled by independent reviewers applying the standards developed by Irene Fountas and Gay Su Pinnell in *Matching Books to Readers: Using Leveled Books in Guided Reading*, Heinemann, 1999.

Licensed By:

TRANSFORMERS RESCUE BOTS

Meet Quickshadow

Adapted by **Brandon T. Snider**

Based on the episode "Plus One" written by
Brian Hohlfeld

LITTLE, BROWN AND COMPANY
New York Boston

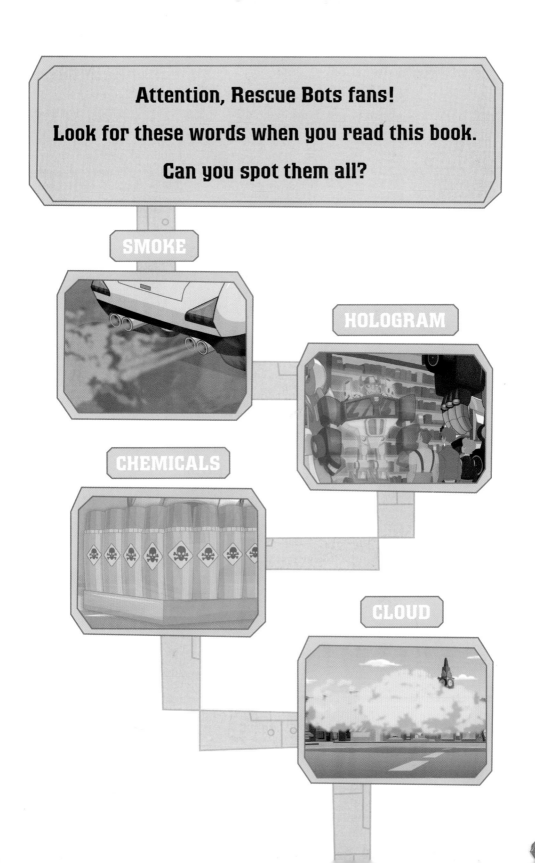

Attention, Rescue Bots fans!
Look for these words when you read this book.
Can you spot them all?

SMOKE

HOLOGRAM

CHEMICALS

CLOUD

This is Quickshadow!

She changes into a sports car.

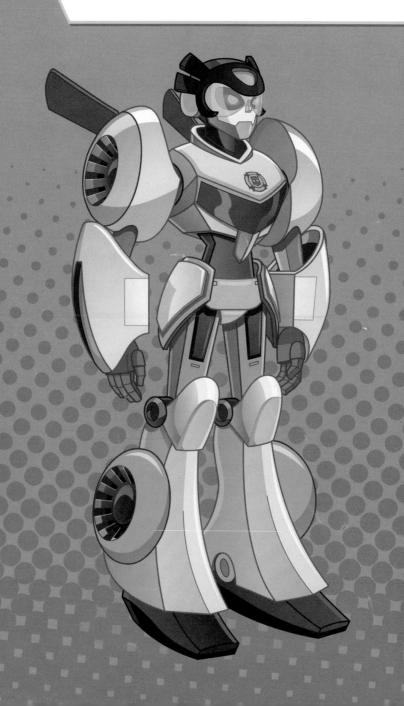

Optimus Prime sent her to Earth
on a mission.
The Rescue Bots are
curious about her.

Blades gives Quickshadow
a tour of their home.

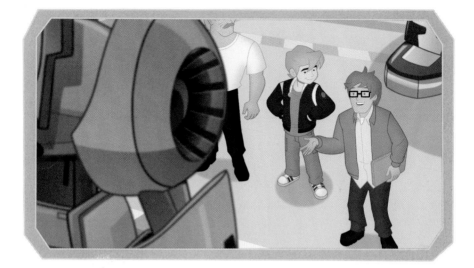

The team has questions.
Quickshadow tells them she
is a secret agent!

Quickshadow uses smoke screens.
She has tire spikes that help
her drive up walls!

Being a spy is lonely.

She is not used to being on a team.

The Rescue Bots will help her.

Dani is excited to meet
a new Autobot!
Heatwave is not so sure.

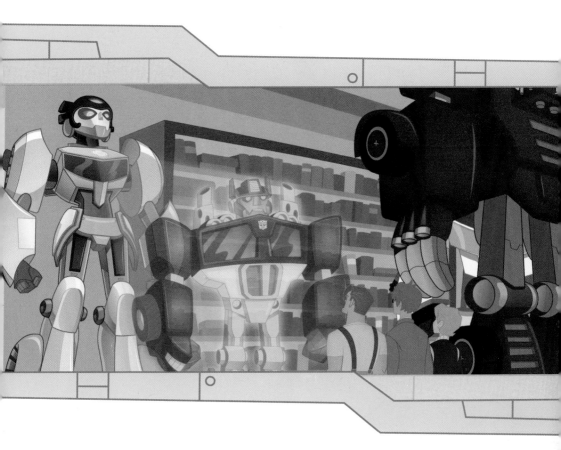

Optimus sends a
hologram message.
The Rescue Bots listen.

"You are a good team,"
Optimus says.
"Quickshadow can help you
be even better."

The Rescue Bots trust their leader.
So they trust Quickshadow.

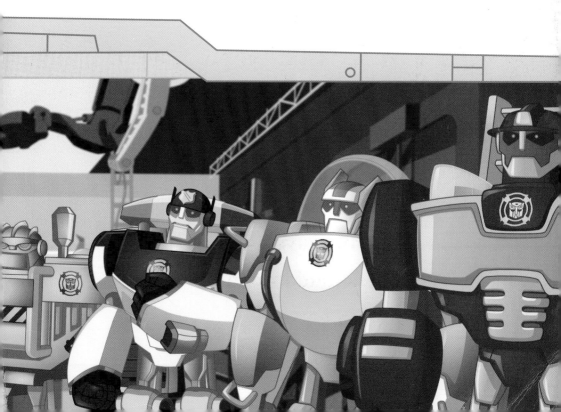

Uh-oh!

A gas station is on fire.

The Rescue Bots roll to the rescue!

Quickshadow watches.

She does not know how to help.

Heatwave sprays foam
on the flaming barrels.
Kade helps.

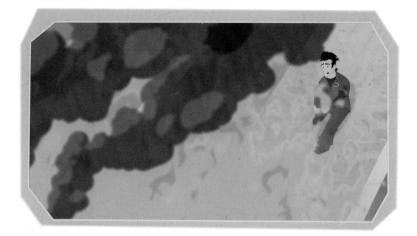

Ernie is trapped!

Boulder can help.

The day is saved.

Later, Doc Greene calls
the Rescue Bots.
They must bring
dangerous chemicals to him.

They must be very careful.
If the cans are damaged,
there could be trouble.

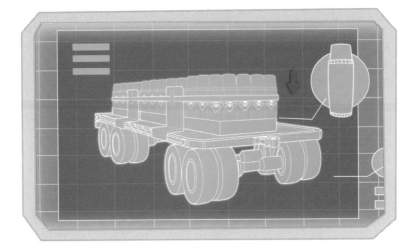

The Rescue Bots
get ready to move.

Heatwave wants Quickshadow
to choose roles for everyone.
This will help her learn teamwork.

Heatwave and Kade
will deliver the chemicals.
Graham and Boulder will clear the path.
Chief Burns and Chase
will handle the streets.

Dani and Blades will watch from above.
The team rolls into action!

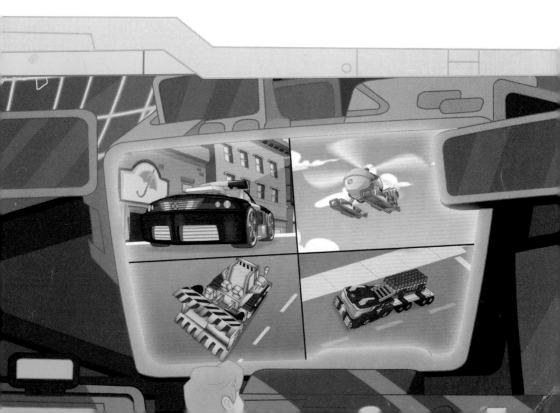

A tree falls in front
of Heatwave.
A can falls.
It smashes open on the street.

An acid cloud escapes.

It is dangerous.

Doc Greene has an idea!

The acid cloud eats everything!
Boulder shovels dirt on the leaking can.

Quickshadow and Cody
arrive with Doc.
Doc made a new chemical
to stop the cloud.

Blades picks up Heatwave
and flies into the sky.

Heatwave sprays Doc's chemical
from the air.
Quickshadow does the same
from the ground.
The acid cloud disappears.

Chief tells the Rescue Bots
they did a great job.
And Quickshadow learned
to work with a team.